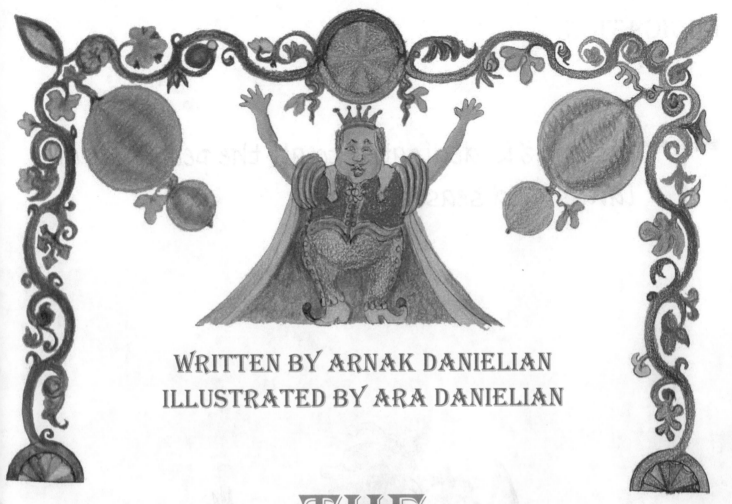

WRITTEN BY ARNAK DANIELIAN
ILLUSTRATED BY ARA DANIELIAN

THE

WATERMELON

KING

DEDICATION

This book is dedicated to all the people on all lands and seas.

Chapter One   THE GRAND FESTIVAL   Page 1
Chapter Two   YOUNG DEAN   Page 4
Chapter Three   KING BRUDERICK   Page 9
Chapter Four   SNOOT SNEEZED   Page 14
Chapter Five   THE INVENTOR   Page 20
Chapter Six   THE WATERMELON KING   Page 26
Chapter Seven   NANI IS MAD   Page 28
Chapter Eight   THE KEY MAKER   Page 33
Chapter Nine   THE TIME KEEPERS   Page 37
Chapter Ten   I'LL BE BACK   Page 42
Chapter Eleven   LOVE POTION   Page 47

CHAPTER ONE

THE GRAND FESTIVAL

The Grand Festival. It was a crowded celebration held once a year. Everyone gathered to listen to the bird keeper. The giant bird on his arm looked at Dean and shrieked!

"Gather around! Gather around everyone, a vision has come to me! Listen carefully! Dark times are coming. Lightnings and rains!

Something gigantic is coming and no one can stop it!"

In the crowd was a young boy named Dean. He had come to the festival to say goodbye to his father, the famous Captain Nicodenus, and Lady Emerald, his mother. Captain Nicodenus was one of the world's best explorers. He had recently designed his new boat, the *Water Dragon*. Only one manufacturer could build such a boat, an old man named Ecko, the most talented boat builder in the country.

Captain Nicodenus was ready for his long journey. In the salty ocean waters the *Water Dragon* awaited, filled with the finest watermelons in the kingdom. The boat set off into the clear waters and soon disappeared behind the hills.

CHAPTER TWO

YOUNG DEAN

Young Dean was left behind with his best friends, a bird named Gul and his dog Pete. He played the flute merrily, all the while thinking about what the bird keeper had said.

People in the kingdom worked very hard. But there was one who never worked, who always enjoyed his life nonetheless: King Bruderick VI. Seated on a soft pillow, drinking the finest juice, and eating all the natural fruits grown in the kingdom, he was enjoying entertainment provided by a troupe of clowns.

King Bruderick thought to himself, *People in my kingdom are workaholics. They work very hard for their gold and silver, which is good for me, because I get to charge them taxes! Speaking of which, isn't it time to collect taxes again? I should ask Nani. She always says yes anyway.*

While the king was wondering how to get more taxes, Dean was making his way home. The sun had set, and his house was filled with shadows.

Dean already missed his dad and his mom, so he went into the house's most interesting room, the captain's room. It was filled with instruments of all sorts, telescopes, books, maps, even a giant anchor. But the object Dean was most curious about was the treasure chest that always remained under lock and key. Dean had never seen what was inside. As he looked closer, he thought he was dreaming.

"Unbelievable!" he said, "the key is in the lock!"

Dean turned the key, as the mechanics of the lock clicked into place.

Atop was a sword engraved with the royal symbols. Beneath that lay a uniform covered with multiple medals.

"Was father a lord? A general? Why didn't he tell me?"

Under the uniform rested a tiny chest. Inside there was a folded handkerchief with his mother's initials on it. He unwrapped the handkerchief. Tucked inside was a large watermelon seed.

"A seed inside a handkerchief?
That's it?"

He placed everything back in its place and went outside to look at the stars. Out of the sky came a deep voice.

"Dean . . ."

Dean looked up. There was a giant old man in the sky. Between his hands was a huge spinning stone. The old man pressed against the stone and stars began to fly out everywhere.

"Look at the other side," said the old man.

On the other side, the sun and the moon appeared at the same time. The light from the planets shone down, and on the ground appeared a watermelon. The dozens of stars began to fill the watermelon, which got bigger and bigger . . . then

everything disappeared, and Dean woke up!

Dean ran back upstairs and opened the chest. He dug out the handkerchief. The seed was still there, but now there was a piece of paper. Drawn on it was a redbird with the words: WAIT FOR THE THREE TWEETS.

Early the next morning, a loud shriek woke up Pete, whose ears perked up. Pete barked, waking Dean. Then there was another loud tweet.

"How many was that?" Dean asked Pete, who barked twice.

"The seed! Hurry! We need to plant it! Follow me!"

The sun was bright, the air was chilly. The scent of flowers was everywhere. It was a perfect morning. Dean, Gul, and Pete got to the planting spot where the magic watermelon had filled with stars. The redbird tweeted a third time, and Dean planted the seed in the ground.

Dean took Pete's water bowl and poured water on the seed.

Instantly, a little bud grew out of the ground.

8

"Wow! The seed is growing already! The sun warms it up, the water wakes it up, and the ground feeds it! We need more water, Pete!" Dean and Pete and Gul rushed off to find more water.

CHAPTER THREE

KING BRUDERICK

In the meantime, King Bruderick VI was yelling at his workers. "Why do you always bring the same food here! What is going on in my kitchen! I will go myself and look at it! Nani! Where are you! Come with me!"

The woman who raised him, Nani, stood up and quickly followed the king to the enormous kitchen.

The main cook, Ilbert, held a giant knife in one hand and a small squealing pig in the other.

"What are you doing?" yelled King Bruderick.

9

"Making vegetable soup with pig for your highness!"

"Freeze!" commanded the king.

The cooks feared the king and hid under the tables.

"Ilbert! Go and count the rice grains in three sacks of rice!" yelled King Bruderick. Ilbert frowned and left to do as he was commanded.

King Bruderick walked up to the little pig. "You look so familiar to me," he said to the pig. "Scribes, write this! From this day on, this piggy will be the royal piggy! I will name you Snoot! And I want Snoot painted on every wall of this kingdom! I know people have not treated you right, Snoot, but you are safe now. Nani, no one gets food for three days in punishment!"

"Bruderick, my little one, your highness, the cooks are not at fault," said Nani.

"At fault? Of course not! But one day they will be at fault for something, right?" answered the king.

"You are always right, but I worry for our subjects," said Nani.

"Nani, I will not allow you to feel worried!" commanded the king. "I will also not allow anyone to eat pig from this day forward. Pig will be our royal symbol of strength. I want Snoot showered, cleaned, dressed, and in my room immediately!"

Back outside, the sun was setting. Dean and his friends had spent all day watering the seed, and the bud had already grown into a small bush.

Dean, Pete, and Gul reached home exhausted. They set a fire in the chimney and sat down to eat soup.

"I have never seen a watermelon seed grow this fast Gul, Pete!" said Dean. "My arms hurt, my legs are killing me, and my hands are about to fall off, but it is still thirsty for water and needs more food. I have to figure something out—and fast!"

Dean woke up early, took his axe, nails, and wood, and created an open pipe leading from the water well. Then he made a giant wooden wheel

with bowls that carried water toward the watermelon bush. Flowers started blossoming from the bush, and one of the flowers quickly grew and became a watermelon. And the watermelon became visibly bigger and bigger.

"That's already a good size to eat!" said Dean, watching it grow. Minutes later, it was even bigger. "Wow, that's bigger than Grandpa's biggest watermelon!" he said. A few minutes after that, it was the size of a small horse. "Shut the water off!" shouted Dean. "It might explode!"

They stopped the water, but then *bang!* Thunder clapped. *Zzzzit!* Lightning struck. The rain began to pour.

Three days and three nights of rain and thunder, the sun rose not from behind the mountains as it usually did, but from behind the giant watermelon! It was enormous!

"I want people from all corners of the land to see and enjoy this watermelon! Go Gul, fly, fly and call everyone!"

Dean rolled up the small message and tied it to Gul's foot.

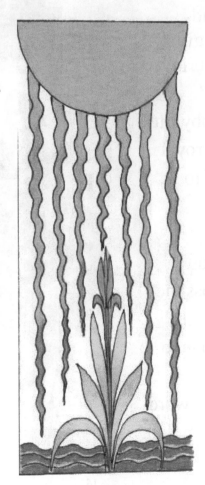

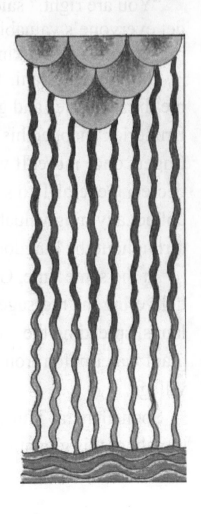

CHAPTER FOUR

SNOOT SNEEZED

Back in the palace the king had called for his general. "General Tito," said King Bruderick, "All my thoughts are marvelous. I think the good people want to pay taxes again. As soon as I thought it, Snoot sneezed once, and then I knew they needed to pay taxes. Then Snoot sneezed twice more, and it was a sign. Now go get my tax money, Tito!" Bruderick snapped his chubby little fingers and pointed at Tito.

"But sire," objected General Tito, "we collected taxes only a month ago!"

"Has it been that long?"

"The people have no more money to pay!" said General Tito.

"You are right," said Nani. "Go get everyone's valuables and present them to the king as gifts!"

"Marvelous, Nani, Tito, bring me the valuables and gifts!" Bruderick snapped his chubby little fingers once more. It was a royal decree. General Tito set off to collect anything valuable throughout the kingdom.

At the same time, Gul was delivering the message across the lands, spreading the word of the giant watermelon from village to village.

Soon General Tito got the word too about this gigantic watermelon.

Shortly after, Tito and his men appeared at Dean's farm and pointed his finger at the watermelon.

"You're the son of Nicodenus. Growing this watermelon for the king, boy?" asked Tito.

"For the people General Tito" said Dean.

"The people are King Bruderick's. The watermelon is the king's! Simple math, boy. Onward, men, take the king's watermelon!" The guards approached the watermelon and pushed and pulled, but the watermelon didn't move an inch.

"Weaklings! Guard the watermelon! It is not to be moved!" Tito commanded his guards as they looked at one another, Tito hurried back to the castle.

Shortly after Tito's arrival back at the castle, Bruderick had found out all about the enormous watermelon. He became very excited. "My trusted General Tito, the point is for me to be happy is it not?"

"Yes, my lord it is."

"Then why am I not smiling?"

"Because the watermelon is not here. My lord, only a handful of my guards were with me. We couldn't move it."

"Excuses! Tito you should know better, you failed me, Tito, and—"

"But, my lord!"

"You dare interrupt me? You not only failed, but you betrayed me! Hamo and Samo, my most trusted heroes. Do not fail me."

"Yes, King Bruderick," replied Hamo and Samo, two giant brothers.

"Seems like I have to do everything myself!" cried the king. "Anyway, Nani, what was I on my way to do?"

"You were going to speak to your father, Bruderick."

"Right!" Bruderick snapped his chubby fingers and walked into an empty room, which had a life size painting of his father Bruderick V.

"Painting of my papa, look at my shiny armor! I am getting ready for battle. Look at me, Papa, I am the perfect modern man. Everyone tries to be like me, isn't that so?"

"My son," a deep voice spoke.

"Agh! What was that?" Bruderick cried, falling backward. "Did you speak, painting of my papa?"

"Yes, it's Papa. Now listen, love is the answer, the answer to all happiness. Listen to my story, Bruderick, my son.

The king loved you and the queen very much . . . this is way before your time. One day, the king and queen wandered off the garden path and got lost. Days later, tired and thirsty, they found a well. An old man had just pulled up a small bucket of water with his last breath, and the king, desperate for water, pushed the old man aside. He fell and didn't get up. The king brought up the bucket of water, but when he turned around, lightning struck his horse. The queen fell down and did not get up. In that moment the king lost his queen, and the prince was born. The king's love turned to pain, and he didn't live long. Remember, son, love and generosity are what should guide all you do."

Bruderick, who had fallen to his knees, stood up and nodded at the painting. "I hear you, papa," he said to the painting and bowed and left.

Meanwhile, Hamo and Samo had reached the watermelon. They looked at each other with confidence and smirked, but the closer they got, the bigger the watermelon became, and their smirks turned upside down. They and all their guards tried to lift it, the watermelon didn't move an inch. Instead their legs got buried in the dirt.

"This is not a watermelon!" shouted giant Hamo.

"This is a water-mountain!" yelled back his brother Samo.

"Snoot and I are waiting for my watermelon!" cried the king. "Where is my wa-ter-me-lon?"

"The watermelon didn't lift up," said Samo.

"Instead the world went down," said Hamo while pointing down.

"Put my world back in place!" ordered the king. "And find the inventor!"

The giant brothers left with their heads down, and in came Houg the inventor.

King Bruderick pointed his finger up.

"When an apple falls from the tree, someone picks it up for me. Houg, my trusted inventor, do not fail me. Bring me the watermelon!"

18

"I will create a device that will pick it up, and a bird that will bring it to you, your highness," said Houg

"What if the bird can't pick it up?" asked Bruderick.

"Then we will bring it by land."

"Tito failed me. Hamo and Samo failed me. Do not fail me!"

"We will bring it to your doorsteps," promised Houg.

"Marvelous!" shouted the king.

CHAPTER FIVE

THE INVENTOR

Houg went and measured the watermelon, and came back to his laboratory. Day and night he calculated and worked until his device was invented. It was a giant mechanism that would lift the watermelon and an even bigger wagon to carry it.

Houg brought together all the carpenters, tree cutters, and builders, and they went to the forest and toiled sunrise to sunset. They worked and worked until finally it was finished.

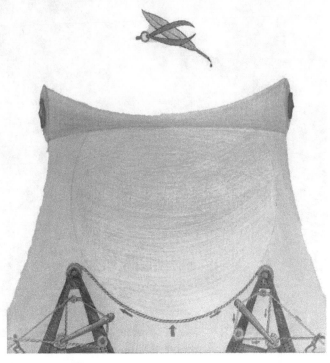

King Bruderick was very impatient. Every day he had looked out his window and watched the watermelon grow. At last his servant came with the good news.

"They are bringing your watermelon, my lord."

Houg brought the country's strongest bulls. Each bull was tied to the next bull with Houg leading the way. And when they got closer to the kingdom wall, General Tito came to let them in.

People gathered around the unbelievable watermelon as Houg pushed forward with his bulls until they reached the giant plaza right in front of the king's castle.

Bruderick, came down to see the watermelon and yelled. "Look, this watermelon looks like me! Unique, unbeatable, and enormous! I shall be on the tippy top when I eat it! I am the watermelon king!" he yelled. The crowd was silent.

"Applause!" Tito commanded, and everyone applauded.

CHAPTER SIX

THE WATERMELON KING

The carpenters attached the lift to the watermelon and began to spin a wooden wheel. Up went Bruderick.

On the top Nani waited, along with his main cook, Ilbert.

His royal tent, table, and his golden utensils were all set.

"You are coming to me, watermelon. I am the watermelon king!" commanded Bruderick.

"I'm ready! Bring me slices from the best parts! And keep bringing it until I say enough!"

"My pleasure," answered Ilbert.

The king ate one piece after the other, without a break.

"More! More! I said more!"

After seeing Bruderick get so big he *did* look like he might explode, Nani commanded. "Guards! The king's life is in danger! Take the king to the palace!" she ordered.

CHAPTER SEVEN

NANI IS MAD

Hamo and Samo appeared with a couple guards and carried the king back to the palace. All the while Bruderick continued to yell, "My watermelon! My watermelon!"

The whole palace was in a panic. The best doctors were brought from all corners of the kingdom, but nothing helped. The country's philosopher looked and said, "This watermelon has a special poison specifically designed to destroy our kingdom. We should bring the watermelon grower immediately. He shall tell us."

Nani ordered the trusted royal guards. "Go bring him and grab him."

"It is better to grab him and *then* bring him," added the philosopher.

Hamo and Samo bowed,

"Shall we punish him and then bring him? Or bring him and then punish him?" asked Tub, the brave knight.

"I know him, and I know his father, Nicodenus. He is an aristocrat," added Samo.

"QUIET!" yelled Nani, pointing at Tub. "You! Tub, bring him to me! I want him to talk!"

Tub hastened to Dean's farm and arrested Dean, Pete, and Gul. He placed them in his armored wagon and took them back to the fortress.

Nani and the philosopher appeared in the dungeon where Dean was held.

"You little troublemaker! You poisoned the king! Now admit that you did it and then rot here!" yelled Nani!

"I didn't do it," answered Dean.

"Then sit and rot here until you admit it!"

"Or rot and then say you did it!" repeated the philosopher.

"He said he didn't do it, so how will we know if he did it or not?" asked Nani. "Release the watermelon to the people, and see what happens."

"You're right!" said Nani. "Do it!"

The crowds rushed forward. People came to eat and eat, slice by slice, but no one inflated. Everyone got full and happy.

"No one got fat," said Hamo

"Should we let Dean free?" asked Samo.

"Someone needs to be at fault here, let it be him! Forget about him. Lock him up with Goug!" commanded Nani.

CHAPTER EIGHT

THE KEY MAKER

During the feast, Dean was in the dungeon. Goug, the dungeon keeper, came closer to the door. "Dean-o, you aren't sleeping, right?"

"Right."

"You want to be my friend, right?"

"Right."

"Okay, a lot of prisoners have tried, but they couldn't resist and fell asleep."

"I won't fall asleep," answered Dean.

"Alright Dean-o, sit and listen to my story, and then you tell it back to me, the same way I told it to you, all right?"

"All right."

Goug brought Dean to his shop, where he began to spin the machine that makes keys. Under the humming noise of the grinding keys, Goug began to tell his story. But Goug spoke so slowly that by the time he got to the next word, people would forget the previous word.

The story that he told was so slow it took three days to tell.

"At the time of this story I didn't exist. My brother Houg did not exist, either. At that time neither of us existed. Only my mother existed.

She was the dungeon keeper, sitting where I am making keys.

They brought in a pirate as a prisoner. In fact the pirate was a captain. The pirate captain's name was Hugog, and he was giant. Mother closed him behind the doors where you are now. Hugog looked in mother's eyes and said, 'Now your eyes will become the ocean I miss,' and he loved mother very much—even more than you can imagine. So much that mother fell in love with Hugog. They loved each other so much that they got married.

They loved each other so much that soon we existed. They loved each other so much that they disappeared from the dungeon into the ocean. There they hid, inside a cave with tons of treasures."

"What about Goug and Houg?" Dean asked with one eye open.

"Ah, you aren't asleep? They fell so in love that they forgot Goug and Houg.
When you are that in love, you forget."

"It was a beautiful story," said Dean, "but they did not forget about you and
your brother. They left you in the palace, because a pirate's life is dangerous."

"Dean-o, you are a better friend than I imagined. Ask me for anything," said
Goug, guiding Dean back into his cell. "Dean-o, your wish is my command. Do
you want me to get you out?"

"No, if you free me, they will punish you."

CHAPTER NINE

THE TIME KEEPERS

Dean took up a small pot of water and glanced at it longingly. "I planted a watermelon, and the king ate it, and the people ate it, and I'm in a locked up cell. Now who can tell me why?"

"I can." The voice came out of the pot, followed by a large head and then a small body.

"Who are you? How did you get inside there?"

"Actually I just got out of here. I am Tik-Tak's grandson, Dip-Tak's son, Hop-Tak, also known as the time keepers. Nice to meet you, Dean."

"I am all ears, Hop-Tak," said Dean.

"A long time ago when King Bruderick VI was a newborn, his father Bruderick V called your father, young Lord Nicodenus, and told him, 'My young knight, you are the bravest and most fair knight in my kingdom. Go from land to land and bring my son a cure, because he doesn't look like a normal child.' Lord Nicodenus did not know where to go, so he came to my father, Dip-Tak for advice. My father heard him out and took him to my grandfather, Tik-

Tak, who was inside a giant pendulum, swinging and thinking, and the giant clock was on the roof, which was spinning and ticking. And the roof was built on walls, which were moving. Long story short, he was inside a giant castle, right on the water, in the center, and the castle itself was a clock. Basically we lived in a clock.

My grandfather and father gave Nicodenus a super watch that brought him to the pyramid of wishes, which lays on dark red water, in which a red-eyed dragon swam. In the center grew a wisdom tree that held all the fruits in the world for all the wishes in the world, and all of that was found in a giant desert. From all around the world people came, with riches to pay off the guards, to come to the tree, and to have their wish granted, for many without riches wished for treasures, and those with riches, wished for more. And barely no one reached the tree. You know why? Because after every step on the red water, closer to the tree, they became more greedy until they sank in the water and became the dragon's food."

"What happened to my father?" asked Dean.

"Getting to the pyramid was one of the hardest tasks he had to face. Very few reached the pyramid, and even those who did could not get to the tree in a hundred years. Your father reached the old judge, who was inside the pyramid, standing on the water. In the judge's hand was the scale of destiny. The old man told him, 'On one side of the scale put your desire, and on the other put what you'll pay for it. If the scale stays even then you may go.' Young Nicodenus answered him, 'I need medicine for a child, and I have this watch to trade for it.' The old man answered him, 'I know, I know. You can pay very dearly for your desire. You can pay with your life. I want the watch very much, but the scale is even without it. You may go,' said the old judge."

"And then?" asked Dean.

"Then, Nicodenus took his first steps on the red liquid, heading toward the tree. And weird thoughts came to his mind. Thoughts that seemed not his own."

"What did the thoughts say?"

"He thought, 'I can have and be whatever I desire once I reach that tree. Perhaps I should become the king, or maybe the king of all kings, the richest and most powerful man in the land.' And then he realized that those thoughts were not his own. Right under his toes swam a giant red-eyed dragon. Nicodenus said out loud, 'Leave me, creature, those thoughts are not mine.' He reached the tree, and when he did, a giant seed fell down from the tree.

Nicodenus understood that this was the cure. In the few days that he spent in that desert, many years had passed outside of the desert.

Old Bruderick V had passed away from pain, and the kingdom was left in Tito's and Nani's hands. Until Bruderick VI reached of age."

"But the seed that I planted did the opposite of saving the king, it punished him!" said Dean.

"Correct, but you, and Bruderick, and I must finish the work that was started by our elders."

"Finish it how?"

"Call your dungeon keeping friend, and ask him to take us to the king."

CHAPTER TEN

I"LL BE BACK

Soon Goug's large nose appeared by the door. "You ready to give me your one request, young Dean-o?"

"I need to see the king," said Dean.

"I'll be back," answered Goug. Not long after this, Goug appeared with Nani.

"So are you ready to talk?" she asked.

"Dip-Tak is a great healer. He needs to see the king," said Dean.

"What he says is true, I am the healer of time," added Dip-Tak.

"If you don't fix the king, you will spend the rest of your life healing in this dungeon!"

"Follow me," said Goug.

They followed him
from room to room, from
corridor to corridor, from
stair to stair until
they reached the room
where the king rested.

"The watermelon, bring
it to me! That's an order!"

Bruderick wiggled his fingers from his bed, unable to move.

"On this land there is no cure for greed," said Dip-Tak.

"Love, my father said, cures all," added Dean.

"Interesting. Does Bruderick love anything?" asked Dip-Tak.

"Watermelon! I love the watermelon!" yelled the king.

Dip-Tak turned away from Bruderick. "Who does he love?"

"He loves me?" suggested Nani.

"I don't love you! I love my Snoot!"

"Take Snoot the piggy to the kitchen. We need to mix him with the watermelon and make him into a liquid," said Dip-Tak.

"No! No one is to lay a hand on my royal piggy!" cried Bruderick.

"It's either the king or the piggy! Pick!" said Dip-Tak.

"The piggy! The king does not matter!" yelled the king bravely.

Nani snapped her fingers. "Grab the piggy and take him to the kitchen." The clown took Snoot to the kitchen.

Dip-Tak went to the kitchen and shortly after returned with a bottle full of red liquid. He handed it to Nani.

"Fill Bruderick's tummy!" said Dip-Tak.

"I will not drink the piggy!" yelled Bruderick. "I want my Snoot back!"

Nani forcefully poured it into his mouth.

Everyone around the king was silent and impatient.

"Did it work?" asked Goug.

"I don't know," said Dean. "Nothing's happening."

Moments later, in front of everyone's eyes, the king began to drop weight.

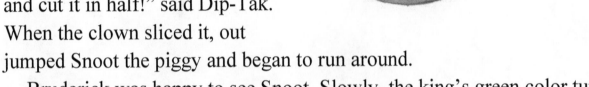

"Bring me a round watermelon and cut it in half!" said Dip-Tak. When the clown sliced it, out jumped Snoot the piggy and began to run around.

Bruderick was happy to see Snoot. Slowly, the king's green color turned normal, and in front of all, he became a tall, handsome king, just like his father.

CHAPTER ELEVEN

LOVE POTION

Bruderick looked in the mirror. "How did this happen?"

"It happens like this: When one loves another more than oneself, the love potion does its job. Nothing comes before love. Love has no barriers. And in a contest, love will always win. In this case, your love potion was simply watermelon juice."

"Thank you all," said the king.

"Thank you, Bruderick, for keeping in your heart the love for the tiny piggy that saved you."

After this, the king treated the people of the kingdom fairly, and he ruled for many happy years.

Dean was freed at last. He returned home to find that his father, Nicodenus, and his mother, Lady Emerald, were missing. He immediately began to search for his family . . . but that's another story.

THE END